Descent is absolutely captivating. Within the first few lines of the story, you will be swirled into a world of rich imagery and intrigue. Once you start reading it, you won't be able to stop with its rich, luscious images that illuminate the senses. As we witness Sona's journey, we are drawn into a world that seems so strange as she seeks to find her own belonging. The story tackles many themes from being accepted for exactly who we are, to the harshness of society when we are different, to how our rights are violated in the name of science. It's a tale of exploration and finding our truth amongst the injustice—very in tune with what is happening in the world right now.

—Cindy Ashton, award-winning TV host, singer, actor, creator of "Liberated," and founder of Brave Voices Rising

Rich and entrancing, *Descent* peels back the layers of growing up "other"—disabled, neurodiverse, marginalized in any way—and lays them bare on a riverbank. *Descent* entwines lush and unflinching storytelling to create a deeply compelling narrative that grips you to the very end.

—Rebecca Burke, editor of *In Between Spaces: An Anthology of Disabled Writers*

In gloriously rich and immersive prose, Deepwater tells the story of Sona, whose "abnormal" body casts her into a life of struggle—and a life of gifts. This confronting tale will have you rooting for its warm and complex protagonist while also reflecting on broader themes of bodily autonomy, disability justice, grief, eco-liberation, and the many routes to resistance and survival. All at once heartwarming and heartbreaking, enraging and hopeful, *Descent* is transcendent.

—Raechel Anne Jolie, author of *Rust Belt Femme*

Arria Deepwater's story *Descent* begins and ends with the body. Deepwater's gift for transmuting sensation into words is present on every page, a portal into the experience of a unique being. Deepwater upends a familiar fish-out-of-water sci-fi trope with every twist of the plot, giving *Descent's* protagonist a bright childhood with a loving mother and an adult life that works well—or well enough. Throughout the story, with delicate and precise language and a vivid sense of place, Deepwater explores the mentality of the colonizer, the meaning of wildness, and the perspective of the non-human living beings in our world. Arria Deepwater is a talent to watch for. I'm looking forward to reading their future work.

—Michelle Ruiz Keil, judge's citation for Omnidawn's Fabulist Fiction Chapbook Contest and author of *Summer in the City of Roses*

Arria Deepwater's *Descent* brings the beautiful and strange alive in language as fluid and sparkling as the water that courses through these pages. A tale that is both pilgrimage and revelation, filled with horror and also renewal, Sona's journey is one that invites us to re-imagine what it means to belong to a body—and from there, to belong to the world.
—Amanda Leduc, author of *Wild Life* and *The Centaur's Wife* and *Disfigured: On Fairy Tales, Disability, and Making Space*

Lyrical, earthy, somatic, even allegorical, *Descent* shines a relentless light on the ways we objectify others, the illusions we harbour of separateness (even from the natural world), and the irrevocable harm we may do as a result. It left me yearning to immerse myself, along with the protagonist, in the earthly, loving, all-enveloping source of our being. An immensely evocative and provocative read, and an ode to mud that is anything but murky.
—Brenda Missen, author of the literary thriller *Tell Anna She's Safe* and the memoir *Tumblehome: One Woman's Canoeing Adventures in the Divine Near Wilderness*

With *Descent*, Deepwater strikes again by creating enduring imagery that rolls along effortlessly, often in just one sentence. A seasoned writer's prose that captures your reader's heart from the first paragraph. *Descent* is well-plotted with developed characters to love and others to revile in a speculative world that is very relatable and accessible. And like any good tale dropping breadcrumbs, Deepwater pulls the reader in on an irresistible ride to the fantastical end. Well done!

—Lorrie Potvin, author of *Horses in the Sand,* and *First Gear: A Motorcycle Memoir,* and winner of Sisters in Crime 2024 Pride Award for Emerging 2SLGBTQIA+Crime Writers

Previous publication

"Undertow" in *In Between Spaces: An Anthology of Disabled Writers*, Stillhouse Press, 2022

Descent

Cover art by Teagan Berard
Cover typeface: Futura

Interior typeface: Baskerville
Interior design by Sophia Carr & Laura Joakimson

Library of Congress Cataloging-in-Publication Data
Names: Deepwater, Arria author
Title: Descent / Arria Deepwater.
Description: Oakland, California :
Omnidawn Publishing, 2025. | Summary:
"Descent is a modern fairy tale, revealing the raw vulnerability and
unseen strength of forging an authentic life from within an
unconventional body. Its edges draw tender shapes often made invisible
by modern society. Within it, the reader is invited to become an
observer to isolation, violation and the magic of secret joy. Each page
weaves a spell of protection around those whose bodies do not
conform-who commit radical acts of rebellion and creativity simply by
daring to exist as their natural selves. Its prose evokes entangled
connections and ever-dissolving boundaries between humanity and the
natural world. In this 2022 Omnidawn Fabulist Fiction Prize winning
story, Arria Deepwater brings an eco-feminist speculative twist to the
growing canon of writers with marginalized identities authoring stories
in their own voices. Those living within the experience of disabilities,
chronic illness, hyper-medicalization, objectification and LGBTQ+ lives
may find some of their truths mirrored back with dark humor, despair,
and a joyful defiance Descent pulses between intimacy and distance,
fluidity and fixed reality, truth and voicelessness. What does it mean
to be real, whole and a part of something wild? And what does it take to
live that fully-in freedom and safety?"-- Provided by publisher.

Identifiers: LCCN 2025013444 | ISBN 9781632431714 trade paperback
Subjects: LCGFT: Fiction
Classification: LCC PR9199.4.D4393 D47 2025 | DDC 813/.6--dc23/
eng/20250331
LC record available at https://lccn.loc.gov/2025013444

Published by Omnidawn Publishing, Oakland, California
www.omnidawn.com
10 9 8 7 6 5 4 3 2 1
ISBN: 978-1-63243-171-4

Descent

Arria Deepwater

Omnidawn Publishing
Oakland, California
2025

To all those who walk the margins. May we find each other and know that we are here together, between worlds.

Sona stepped naked from her tent, ready to dig the hole. Having chosen a spot by the river that afternoon, she went directly to it and began by moving a few small rocks away. She'd been careful to map the terrain in her mind, knowing that once night fell around the site, small dangers might wrap themselves in darkness. But she was lucky; the moon was feeling friendly and willing to help. The breeze touched her skin lightly, stirring it like a sea of sensation. She felt her body as a whole, not as separate parts, but as a single organ. Trees huddled close around her, stretching their arms toward the night sky. The air smelled of moving water and damp moss; lichen crawled across the craggy surface of a nearby rise, cradling its algae symbiont, tucked unseen within its tiny moisture-dipped ruffles. To Sona, it seemed as if the forest itself was watching, encouraging her.

She used her hands like paddles, digging with gentle persistence. Beginning, as always, by trusting the ending. The hole would measure no more than two feet across and be just as deep, needing about an hour to complete. Sona moved the soil through her hands, sinking into a state beyond thought. As she dug, her body readied itself. Her blood slowed, seeming to thicken in her veins, and her awareness stretched along the full expanse of her lengthening breaths. Her senses relaxed open and the night pushed in, bringing with it a symphony of communication. Sona felt the micro-organisms pulsing in the cool, damp earth, the sap, barely awake, seeping beneath the cambium of the trees. She could smell the way the moonlight traced the feathers of a nearby owl, the shape of its dangerous beauty. Scent trails and tiny electromagnetic tendrils imprinted themselves onto her awareness through her skin. And Sona dug.

She felt the first contractions, deep within tissues now engorged and slick, and moved to squat over the hole, forearms braced against her knees—palms turned upward. Raising her eyes to the full moon, Sona stretched her upper body skyward, mimicking the trees. The sound began deep in her belly, rumbled up through her throat, and resonated in the sinus cavity behind her nose. Her skin tingled, every synapse in her body sparked, and she felt the first egg, round, soft and slippery, slide from inside her to land sweetly in the hole. Egg after egg passed as she sung them from her belly into the nest. Each one sent waves of tingling, electric pleasure through her pelvic girdle, the nerves in her brain answering with flashes of blue and yellow light. Small blisters, stimulated by the digging, filled with fluid; fine lines of throbbing pustules rose to the surface of her hands. Eventually, her song changed, becoming lighter, the pitch modulating higher. Shifting her weight back, Sona looked at the nest. Her consciousness could not count the more than thirty eggs, but her whole being, all the spaces

18

between her cells, felt filled with deep satisfaction.

Delicate blue speckles on pale yellow, glistening in the moonlight. She placed her hands gently on the eggs and poured sound into the nest. The skin on her fingers and palms became as thin as gauze and gelatinous fluid gushed onto the eggs, permeating their still porous surface, feeding them.

When it was over, Sona let out two quiet sounds, the throaty chirps merging gracefully with the murmur of the river. She used her feet and legs to carefully push the wet soil over the eggs. Only after the nest was well covered and camouflaged did she slowly stand and move cautiously into the cold river. She had a spot alongside two large rocks in the near-centre where she could surrender to the rush of the spring surge while staying nestled in place. The layer of earth clinging to her body melted away with the current and her skin began to absorb the water, especially through the slack flesh of her hands. Floating at the surface, she felt the moon look at her body, felt the river cool the inflamed places.

For a moment she was Sona, as she was meant to be. She belonged with each breath, and as the river caressed her body, she returned slowly to her more human self. Despite the chill in the water, she was not cold, but she was tired. Deeply tired; aware, all at once, that she craved the comfort of flannel, the embrace of sleep.

Sona stretched languidly as she stepped out of the water,

her muscles sore and her skin tender under the moonlight. It was then that something bit her. Angry and stinging, it sunk into the flesh at the back of her left thigh and she fell. Everything went dark. No moon or stars, no flicker of a dream.

20

As a child, Sona was attracted to cool, wet places. If her mother turned her back for more than a moment on rainy days, Sona would dash for the garden, curling herself amongst the hostas. From infancy, her skin was flaky, sloughing off in small patches, and her mother agonized over how to keep her moisturized.

Through trial and error, she learned that prescription, over-the-counter, and homemade concoctions were of little use. In some cases, they clogged her daughter's sensitive skin to the point of causing infection. From some combination of desperation and invention, she discovered that if she allowed Sona to soak in the bath for at least an hour a day, this did more than anything else to keep her skin healthy.

Sona began moulting when she was five years old. From then on, every autumn, she would develop a high fever, begin sweating, and become lethargic. Over the course of a few days, her skin would change texture across her whole body, and her mother tenderly exfoliated it. She stood Sona in the bathtub with a bucket of water and plugged the drain. From head to toe, she caressed Sona in small gentle circles using a soft towel. Down her face and arms, her chest and belly, her back, and all the way to the soles of her feet, rinsing the cloth as needed. Relaxing, Sona would hum and murmur until the bucket was coated in gauzy film and the bottom of the bathtub was littered with shiny flakes.

When she was nine, Sona felt the first stirrings of a deep yearning for solitude during her moulting time, but had not known how to ask. Three years later, when her mother was unable to take time off work for their ritual, she found herself with an opportunity. Despite her mother's stern instructions to abide by the routine, as soon as she was alone in the house, Sona filled the bottom of the bathtub with cool water and climbed in. For hours, she lay in the tub, half sleeping, half dreaming, until rather absentmindedly, she scratched at her scalp and realized she could work the skin away in long fragments—like peeling a piece of fruit.

When she was finished, she sat cross-legged, holding the moult in her lap, and allowed herself to feel the full depth of her instincts. Humming quietly, water licking the tops of her legs, Sona methodically, lovingly, ate her discarded skin. She felt energized, better than during any previous moulting. She never told her mother, pretending instead that she had followed through with the ritual, just as they always had. After that, Sona insisted on moulting in private, and her mother tried to accept this as a natural part of growing up.

Sona's childhood was marked by patterns of isolation. She was quiet by instinct and seemed only to bond over shared endeavours. Saturday morning art class meant social activity, but Sona had difficulty translating these connections to birthday parties and play dates, feeling disoriented by the swirling points of stimulation, the need to adapt to changing circumstances rather than focus on the task at hand. Swimming was both a saving grace and a challenge. Not at all able to tolerate the chlorine of the local community centre's pool, Sona waited for spring to arrive, when her mother might successfully claim one of the coveted spots in the half-day swim camp that ran out of the small municipal beach. An ebb and flow of disparate feedback drifted home to Sona's mother on a raft of notes.

"Sona displays genuine talent for swimming and enjoys the activities!"
"Sona has been very distracted and is having trouble listening. She prefers to float by herself and not participate."
"Sona is very patient with the less skilled children. She's a great help!"
"Sona has had difficulty relating to the other campers."

Sona felt the sting of living as an outsider—of being teased, rejected, or criticized—but also felt the warmth of praise and small encouragements keenly. And she did not need to speak her feelings for her mother to trace their shape. Tiny muscles in Sona's jaw would flicker when she felt upset; heightened stress moved through her nimble body as a fluid tremor, sending her skittering to her room, where she would renew herself with drawing or dance or simple rest. Joy often came in the form of quiet tears, and while she did not laugh much, Sona could dissolve into puddles of giggles when embracing silly moments. Her mother, having deepened her trust in her child's open nature, realized there was not much for her to do, but watch, and respond as needed.

As the years passed, Sona grew tall and lithe, her body remaining almost straight, her silhouette barely curving from waist to hip to thigh. Puberty seemed to skip her, almost in its entirety. She had strong supple muscles, and her limbs were slightly smaller in proportion to her lengthy torso. Her fingers were long and elegant, with pads that rounded out around nails that never really seemed to grow. Her skin had a golden tinge and swam with something dusky underneath. She had eyes the colour of sand, rimmed in dark bands. Her hair was the colour of rich soil and grew in gentle curls that she wore short over her ears, neither quite girlish nor boyish.

At seventeen, she had not yet menstruated and she had no noticeable breasts. Her mother took her to a gynecologist who, upon inspection, referred her for a pelvic ultrasound, the results of which were declared to be "quite interesting."

For over a year, she was shuffled between one specialist and another. Sona began to suspect that doctors, as a tribe, may be a strange and maladapted people. She observed them as closely as they pored over her charts and test results, as they poked and prodded in tender places. Each one seemed to exist inside a kaleidoscope of misplaced emotions, swirling through enthusiasm, fascination and resentment in their own time and at their own rhythm. They said the oddest, most startling things, expecting her to act as a mirror for their outbursts and conclusions. They displayed her to students as if she were a specimen, dissected and pinned. Test results baffled them, quickly curdling their interest into indignation, filling the air with a sour, chalk-like film that coated the back of Sona's throat.

A flat cubist rendering of Sona's body emerged and she felt smaller and less real the more details were added to it. She was told that, from the exterior, she appeared to have female genitalia. However, the examination revealed a shorter-than-average vagina, a malformed cervix, and a uterus that was shaped more like a banana than an upside-down pear, lined on either side by a series of small, almost inconspicuous lumps. She was diagnosed as infertile; hormonal therapy was discussed as one option, surgery as another.

Sona felt captured in bytes of information and digital images. Data linked together, piece by piece, with invisible barbed wire, pulling apart her emotions the more she reached for them, leaving her sense of self pock-marked with lesions, red with welts. She began to experience waves of panic, anxiety that seized her throat from within and twisted her chest into painful knots the size of golf balls.

Into this fractured landscape, the dream began calling Sona into something new. In the dream, it was always the same. It came first as a song, a resonating pulse that soothed and carried Sona in its currents. Everything elongated along convex lines, as if she was looking at the world from inside a bubble. And always, there was the call to move beyond thought into mud, into water, into clouds of blue and yellow light. Sona floated in the dream, safe and certain.

But in the waking world, every part of her body noted and catalogued by the doctors, it became more and more difficult to see herself through her own eyes. It became harder to feel herself in her own body. So she followed the dream, listened for the song that called her, and her heart began to know the way. She opted to live with her condition as it was, leaving the doctors to puzzle over what records they had.

Not long after, Sona discovered her gills and knew enough to keep them secret, even from her mother. They began as three discreet lines on either side of her ribcage, just below her armpits. Over the course of several months, they deepened into lacy fissures covered by strong flaps of skin. Sona spent hours in the bath learning how to use them. Her body took almost a year to adjust. The process was sometimes painful and embarrassing, but Sona loved her gills more than anything. She relearned how to swim in the presence of others—remembering to surface in a timely manner so as not to arouse either interest or alarm.

In early spring of her twenty-second year, the dream puddled in her cells until she began to feel its supple presence even while she was awake. Her senses heightened, allowing the slightest change in the breeze, the lightest touch of rain, to dance in places deep within her body. Different than her autumn moult, which tingled with a heat that tired her, desire melted across the surface of her skin. Without direction towards any person, it called her instead towards the woods. To melt-soaked moss and lichen dripping from the face of rocks still bracing from winter's chill. To the pulse of water pushing against its banks, wondering if its shape could hold. That first time, Sona felt uncertain and confused. Driven by instinct and discovery, she would remember the laying as a collage of patchwork memories. The awkward and messy stitched alongside the dazzling and ecstatic. She had been through three cycles since then. This had been her fourth.

S ona woke on the ground, mud once again clinging to her skin. Rolling gently from her side to her back, she felt her mind moving slowly. She stretched her limbs gingerly, pulled herself up on her elbows, then her hands and, with effort, into a sitting position. She rubbed the back of her left thigh, where she had been bitten, and found a lumpy inflammation, tender to the touch; without thinking, her hands began to explore the rest of her body. When she reached her right ear, a blistering pain stabbed along the nerves. Gasping, she quickly pulled her hand away. Her ear continued to throb hotly while her surroundings came into focus, the sharp edge of pain slicing through the fog in her mind. She looked at the sky. The moon wasn't as high as it had been but was still clearly visible. It had no answers for her. Darkness opened mutely around it, what few stars there were hid whatever they had seen in raw light. Not much time had passed.

Carefully, she probed her ear with her fingers, caught for a moment in frozen horror. She had been pierced. A cold, metal bolt. A small flat nut on either side. A rectangular piece of metal hanging from it, about half the size of her pinky. Beneath her fingers, Sona could feel something etched into its surface.

Her heart thundered, adrenaline overtaking any lingering effects of sedation. She trembled slightly and

31

concentrated on taking slow, steady breaths, feeling the damp soil beneath her body and reaching gently for inner calm. She searched for something familiar—anything familiar. The shape of the large rock she used to guide herself into the water, even in the deep dark. The bitter comforting smell of pine. The feeling of a slight breeze, tumbling down from somewhere up-mountain.

And then.

Above the constant murmur of the river, a hush in the bushes on the opposite shore. Sona turned her head in the direction of the noise, wincing as acrid pain showered her face, neck and shoulder. It could have been the wind or the innocent movement of an animal. And it might have been whispering or the rustling of bodies. Sona could see nothing in the dark, nearly shapeless shrub to give a clue as to the truth.

She waited, naked, terribly aware that exposed as she was by the silver light of a clear full night, if anyone was out there … they could see her. Sona strained to listen as her flesh tightened and the rocks pressing into her palms felt dead cold, lifeless. She willed herself to look away from the noise, to look at the moving river and trace the line of trees against the sky, and tried not to panic as her breath rasped past the fear clawing at her throat. She needed to move. She needed to find the place within her that knew how, but the blood rushed through her veins so fiercely now that it dissolved all thought.

32

Instinctually, she bent her head towards the pain in her ear, and the incandescent flash of sensation stirred her capacity to focus.

Slowly, Sona pivoted onto her hands and knees and crawled back to her tent, aware of, or imagining, the weight of a malevolent gaze resting on her back. She moved deliberately. Again and again, the impulse to run mindlessly into the wild snapped through her consciousness, and repeatedly she struggled to maintain composure. Forest debris pushed sharply into her skin, making her knees sting and the still delicate flesh on her hands prickle with discomfort. She struggled to keep her breathing steady, small cries catching in her throat, but she used the pain to sharpen her mind, to warm her aching muscles. Her body, now covered in a cold sweat, was beginning to stiffen, and she strained to keep her senses alert to the environment around her.

She fumbled with the tent flap. Her fingers struggled to stay in control, the zipper clenched its teeth against her efforts. Finally, crossing the threshold and wrapping herself in the sleeping bag—putting even the flimsiest of boundaries between herself and whatever was out there—Sona was flooded with a relief so sweet it almost overwhelmed her. She had no way of knowing how long she sat there. Curled over, her muscles shaking with tremors, her forehead pressed into the tent floor. It felt like centuries. A shapeless void without time. But somewhere inside of it a light of awareness flashed, yellow and blue. She had to get dressed. Like she had needed to get to the tent.

Still shaking in waves, tremors undulating up and down her body, Sona moved her head and reached for the flap, folding it back cautiously. A small triangle of forest opened beyond, indifferent to the threat that may be sheltering within it. She watched for a moment and then a moment more, but there was no movement. No one slunk from the bushes towards her tent. She pulled herself upright and took the deepest breath she could manage, and then another. Not wanting to turn on even her headlamp, she felt for her clothes in the dark. Trembling, Sona dressed without light, sneaking tiny glances outside. Nothing she saw reassured her. The trees still stood, the river still flowed. Its constancy did not mock her, but she felt deceived. The belonging she had known lay raw and dismembered under the starlight. The skin of comfort pulled back to reveal a foolish delusion.

By the time she was dressed, the tremors had calmed and her breathing had grown steady. There was no sign of her attackers, no signal that they lurked in the shadows. She began to gather her things, packing methodically, daring a little light from her headlamp smothered in a sweater. It was not possible to collapse the tent properly in the dark, and neither was it safe to try the trail, slick with spring mud and snarled with roots. She huddled just inside, flap open, her sleeping bag wrapped around her shoulders and her utility knife clutched in her hand, determined to stay watchful until morning.

Hours passed. Her body ached with a pulsing stress, and fatigue dragged at her senses like a weight tied to rope in the deep ocean. The pain in her ear was ceaseless, and each time she felt herself nodding off, she would twitch towards it, its sharp edges shredding the dullness stealing into her mind. It may have helped if she could have thought about anything beyond the need to stay awake, to watch the trees and the water. Her mind was clear enough to know what to do, but not free enough to consider what had happened. All of her awareness was pinned to the moment, under a dread that flattened her feelings and stole her thoughts before they had a chance to show themselves.

Shortly before dawn, when the edges of the night were barely beginning to soften, Sona roused herself and dug her first aid kit out of her pack. She dabbed gently at her ear with hydrogen peroxide, hearing the bubbles foam. The cloth came away bloody.

Again, her eyes scanned the tree line and her ears listened for any noise that didn't belong, and still there was nothing. She pinched either end of the bolt as best she could and pulled. The pain sent shards of white light flashing behind her eyes. The bolt didn't budge, but Sona continued to try until there was enough light to finish packing up and she could head down the trail safely. Before leaving her campsite, she took a furtive glance in the direction of the nest. It looked undisturbed, but she couldn't tell for certain. Not wanting to reveal it to anyone who may still be watching, she chose to leave without checking on her eggs. She could only hope that whomever had done this hadn't seen her laying.

The hike was long, but the movement did her muscles and her mind good. As her limbs moved her through the forest, the exhaustion loosened its hold. By the time Sona reached the rental car, she could feel the outlines of her self again, and the security of not being followed. As clarity reasserted itself, however, a growing spectre of doubt clung to her shoulders. She tossed her pack into the trunk and dropped into the seat behind the wheel, the doubt sliding in beside her, sucking the oxygen from the cabin.

Sona folded herself around the fear she felt and looked into the rearview mirror. Her right ear glared back at her. Its upper half was swollen and bruised, blood crusted in the folds like shadow taken form. A tag—ugly and utilitarian—hung from the bolt piercing its very centre, and as she had suspected, it was stamped. Gingerly, she leaned forward, tilting the tag so she could read it. On the side facing outward was a seven-digit code. A senseless string of numbers and capital letters, in large block print. She took her phone out and, after a few failed attempts, was able to get a picture of the reverse side. In much smaller lettering, it read, "North Pacific U, Dept of Zoology."

Sona leaned back into her seat. She considered driving straight to the police but felt unsure how her story would be received. The whole thing sounded unbelievably bizarre to her, and she could still feel her ear throbbing, see the tag hanging from it. There was also the growing urge to protect her nesting site. If she went to the police, surely they would visit the spot where it all happened. What if they found her eggs? Eventually, amidst the questions and fear, one fierce truth broke through. She felt angry.

Riding that feeling, Sona was determined to confront her attackers directly. As she drove to the university, her thoughts were razor sharp. Emotions swirled around them and fell away bleeding, viscera exposed. She tried to stay focused on the feel of the road slipping beneath the car, the grip of the steering wheel under her hands. When she arrived, resonating with agitation, Sona presented herself to a reedy, bland-looking woman who apparently spent her days stationed at the zoology department administration desk.

After several minutes of unsuccessfully demanding to see someone in charge, Sona pointed to the tag on her ear and demanded instead to see someone who could tell her about it. The woman's face brightened slightly as she stood and leaned over the desk to get a good look at the tag. She punched the code into her computer and responded with an administrator's enthusiasm at having located the correct information. Sona was directed towards an office three doors down the hall on the left, bearing a plate embossed with the title "Department Head." Inside, she found a middle-aged man sporting a greying ponytail and glasses clipped over the neck of a limp T-shirt, which was tucked haphazardly into ill-fitting cargo pants. His excitement upon seeing her was palpable. Sona's rage and violation were thwarted at every turn by his abject exhilaration.

"Oh yes! You see we have to tag you in order to follow your condition and habits. It's very important that we keep track of these things. There is a tiny device imbedded in the tag that serves as a sensor and a transmitter. With it, we can monitor your movements, your body temp and heart rate, even some of your hormonal shifts."

While he spoke, the professor rifled through various files on his desk, his words picking up pace as his search became more frenetic. "The study has been years in development. There are very specific parameters. We have to collect data on each living specimen for at least an entire year before—Ah! Here it is!"

He held a thick file aloft and presented it to Sona. It contained copies of articles from medical journals, fully illustrated and annotated. Repulsed, she realized she was looking at photographs of her naked body, years younger, her face obscured by black bars. He shuffled the papers as she held the file open and there, on display, were images of her reproductive organs, straight from her ultrasound report.

"Until now we only had the reports and articles from years ago. It took some doing to find out your identity, let me tell you! And then, of course, we had to locate you. We were so excited to find that you lived nearby. It makes everything easier."

Sona snapped the file shut and tossed it onto his desk, insisting that the bolt be removed or she would have it removed herself. The professor bristled visibly but pressed on, "No, no. That's entirely impossible."

He held his hands up as if helpless. "No one can remove it. Your species has been declared critically endangered. It's illegal to interfere with approved conservation efforts." The professor took a deep breath, made a visible effort at relaxing his shoulders, and spoke carefully, "Anyone who removes that bolt will face serious fines and possibly jail time."

The words hung in the air for a moment before they slithered below Sona's rib cage and sunk deep into the pit of her stomach. She felt deflated and heavy, exhausted beyond measure, and had barely begun to grapple with what the professor was saying when he laid a hand gently on her arm and said in a reassuring tone, "In order to optimize the success of our breeding program, it's vital that we track your behaviour in the wild."

Sona, motionless, felt tentacles of horror crawling through her organs and up her spine.

"We have a captive specimen here in the Aquatic Observation Lab. Would you like to see?"

In a daze Sona allowed herself to be guided through a labyrinth of hallways and stairwells. As they passed through a set of double doors, unlocked by his key card, a slight odour of mildew crept into her nostrils. They stood on a small landing bisecting a set of stairs. The professor directed Sona to the upper floor and, with a flourish, invited her to look at a large marine observation area. Excitedly, he explained that the site had originally been built to house river otters, but it had been adapted for this special breeding program. Sona peered over the railing, her eyes scanning the simulated rocky terrain, dotted with trees and shrubs. The artificial shore arched in a semicircle around a deep pond of water. He prattled on about the facility, explaining that the observation deck on the level below had a large window that allowed for a full underwater view of the pond. She watched, unable now to look away, as he extended a slender finger and hunched towards her, whispering conspiratorially, "There she is."

Sona saw a woman whose skin, obviously stuck in a phase of incomplete moulting, had gone sallow and waxy. Her hair was stringy and fell out in raggedy clumps. She was older than Sona, but it was impossible to tell by how much because her face was sunken, her body thin with exhaustion. Her mouth and jaw were peculiarly wide and her eyes, filled with deep confusion and loneliness, were set noticeably farther apart than normal. The woman in the tank raised her chin and made two short croaking noises that came out as a strangled wheeze. Sona's stomach lurched, bile and empathy threatening to pour out of her uncontrollably.

The professor's voice, barely audible, hissed with heated emotion. "She has no human speech." Sona did not remember leaving the facility, only the feeling of her legs pumping wildly as she ran.

S ona had never grown to like the busyness of the outside world. She navigated high school through a series of art clubs and yearbook layouts, lunches eaten mostly alone in a quiet classroom and prolonged absences enriched by independent studies. Teachers liked her quiet persistence and often felt more comfortable accommodating her simple requests than complicating their lives by struggling to integrate her more fully.

Under the practical direction of a guidance counsellor and the impassioned support of an art teacher, Sona was able to secure a place in a fine arts program with a focus on illustration and animation. The studio work allowed her to use her time and energy well while deflecting the usual pressures to socialize. After first year (two semesters spent in a dorm, sharing a room, and adapting to the limited facilities by placing a large tote bin under the shower and folding her body into it), she moved into her own small apartment. There she used the bedroom as a dedicated studio and allocated the main space as her living area. She flowed through her days with stained fingers and far-away eyes.

Being seen as an artist, Sona discovered, suited her. She sloughed off any pretense of normality, embracing creative eccentricity. It was a way for others to make sense of what they experienced when they interacted with her. Sona felt vaguely affirmed by it, but more than that, she felt settled within it, calmed.

During her second year, Sona stumbled into selling custom home and pet portraits in warm, whimsical, freehand styles. Her customers craved her ability to drip their everyday reality in light that seemed to come from another world, to set their domesticated lives inside a natural space crowded with wild magic.

Sona's work—both personal and academic—explored moments of transformation and invited the viewer to perceive from multiple varied perspectives. One sculptural project used different lenses set at various angles to magnify or contract, distort or expand, a hyper-realistic, cluttered, miniature living room in the process of being packed (or unpacked). A textile class produced a large macramé wall-hanging that melted highly structured, monochromatic patterns into tangled masses of chaotic colour. At home, she worked on four-by-six-foot panels of mixed media depicting abstract spacial boundaries— blurred lines between solids and liquids—dancing in endless shades of blue and yellow. Or smaller pieces that played with the way the mind sees the natural world, distorting the proportions until the centre of vision appeared larger while the periphery stretched around curved edges. The dream pursued Sona, erupting into her work again and again. She did not run from it, but stood open, seeking it as purposefully as it came

44

to her. Learning to capture its rhythm and nuance gave her work a quality of the uncanny, seeping into her portfolio in ways people responded to without really knowing why.

Sona's mother missed her daughter, but they spoke regularly. Their weekly online visits gave her mother a chance to ask Sona whether or not she'd found a place to swim, listen to her talk about her current projects while she scanned them with the camera, and try to avoid encouraging her too much to connect with her peers. She relaxed into the stories of Sona discovering her joy for wild swimming in the cold waters of inland lakes and rivers, even though the group that met to do it never seemed to yield any friendships. She sighed with relief when the calls focusing on Sona's work ended with a tale of a professor's encouragement or coffee with a classmate to discuss the assignment. It was more difficult for her mother to trust in Sona's contentment from a distance. She was less able to detect the small changes in muscle tension, the daily tone of her voice, or the shifting waves of mood. So she collected the small moments of happiness in her daughter's life like beach glass, holding them to the sun, watching the light warm them.

Just weeks before graduation, Sona received a phone call from a long-time neighbour back home. Her mother had collapsed in the grocery store and been pronounced dead of a ruptured aneurysm at the hospital.

"She had only just been diagnosed, Sona. She would

have told you, but she was waiting for more information. She needed to know if she could fly out to see you for graduation—oh! It's all just so sad."

Sona felt deeply woven threads holding part of her life together begin to fray even before she had disconnected the call. She had projects to finish, but discussing the issue with her professors seemed impossible. As a task, it was shrouded in thick mist and separated from her by a chasm of teeth-like craggy rocks made of despair. Not knowing how to navigate, she chose a simple path. Spend money she had saved to fly home for a handful of days, set details in motion—delaying any organized gatherings—and return to school temporarily.

When she did, people noticed the change in her. Rather than focused on something only she could see in the distance, Sona's eyes seemed to look for something nearby. Something vaguely threatening. A few approached her gently, enquiring, but the final weeks of school were frenzied for everyone. It was easy to disguise her grief in layers of paint and fluid, digitized images.

Friends of her mother texted and emailed. Sona forced herself to answer, but she could not manage much more than a series of clipped generalities. Arrangements were not as difficult to make as they might have been. Her mother, Sona knew, had purchased a full funeral and interment package. They had discussed it, it had all been settled. She relied heavily on these instructions—the almost too calm, overly quiet, support of the funeral directors. Things were set for a service and reception in mid-June. Contact was made with her mother's estate lawyer. Here too, her mother had prepared the way for things to be as uncomplicated as possible.

What Sona truly struggled with was how to manage the transition in her own life while adjusting to the looming void in the shape of her mother. Before her mother's death, Sona had interviewed for a few jobs, unsure of what she actually wanted. It was possible for her to support herself with her own work, at least for a while. She had considered building a freelance illustration and animation business, but suddenly she felt untethered. Her energy consumed by the mundane activities of daily living and the near feverish completion of her degree, Sona's thoughts dissolved; attempts to plan slipped through her fingers like sand.

The dream called her into spaces that abided no thought, that swaddled her in feelings of belonging without connection, home without location. In this haze, a job offer arrived. Junior Concept Designer for a small creative gaming and app studio. Despite its proffered flexibility and independence, the job resonated with an organizational force that tugged at Sona. Considering it, she felt the broken threads knitting themselves around something dense and helpful, drifting pieces falling into orbit around it.

She accepted the position, negotiating a slightly delayed starting date that would give her time to address the necessities at her mother's and return with a short break. Sona completed the last of her art projects and retreated into her own apartment, packing everything in less than three days, giving notice to her landlord, and then getting on a flight.

When she needed a distraction, she searched online for her next apartment. More than once, she hovered above the keypad on her cell, wondering about rescinding the declaration to vacate her apartment. There was no immediate need to move—other than the ache in her heart, the pull to shed one stage of life and step into another. The offices of her new job were located near the northern limits of the city, nestled in foothills festooned with industrial complexes, outdoor shopping centres, and townhouse communities connected by a circuitous tangle of streets and thirsty grass boulevards. She would need transportation if she stayed in her apartment, but buying a car rather than moving certainly had its advantages.

Then she found a posting for a bright spacious one-bedroom in a small town up the coast from the city. Sona had been there with her wild swimming group and had admired its proximity to the marshes. It was one of those quaint old fishing villages that could have collapsed and fallen into the sea. Instead, it had survived by nurturing ecotourism, higher-end shoreline homes for commuters and artisanal craft businesses that could cater to newcomers and seasonal visitors while still being supported by the full-time residents. Sona had enjoyed the laid-back community vibe, but she could imagine herself there because of the deep wandering estuary that stretched its fingers far inland, the water losing its salty tang the farther it travelled from the ocean. Even in winter, she would be able to get on her bike and, within ten minutes, be wending her way along dirt trails hugged by sleepy trees, the smell of damp fertile sanctuary filling her lungs.

The apartment was an easy walk to the train station, which conveniently connected with another near enough to work, about an hour's ride away. Because the company supported remote participation, she could limit her appearances to a few times a month. In between taking most of her mother's clothes and kitchen items to a women's shelter, navigating awkward run-ins with co-workers and neighbours, and otherwise tending to all of the essential and strange rituals of death—both reverential and bureaucratic— Sona paid a deposit and chose paint colours. She would wake up from sleep, sorrow and fatigue saturated by the dream, and immediately envision how she would set up her new space.

I gnoring the professor's warning, Sona made a concerted effort to rid herself of the tag. Multiple attempts to wrestle with the nuts on either end of the bolt using needle-nose pliers resulted only in a swollen and bruised ear. She tried exposing it to a magnet, but the electronics appeared to be shielded. She approached a local metalworker, but upon seeing the tag, both she and her partner refused to remove it. Her investigations into the possibility of hacking the tag revealed that, while not thoroughly impossible, the reputable tech professionals wouldn't override the university's code. The disreputable sorts, lurking in unpleasant corners of the internet, demanded payment beyond the reach of either Sona's capacity or conscience.

For the next several months, Sona did everything she could to stay in her apartment. Making the shift to a fully virtual arrangement with work was easy enough. Leaving her home was a necessity from time to time, but each excursion into the world left Sona shaky and bone tired. Despite the ability to track her remotely, there was no mistaking the evidence that she was being followed. Sometimes, she would catch a small movement out of the corner of her eye and turn to see someone scribbling in a notepad. Other times, people with clipboards and binoculars would brazenly watch her from a coffee stand while she moved amongst the stalls in the farmer's market. Without thinking, Sona would raise her hand to her ear and feel the cold metal of the tag, the skin around it prickling.

She deeply missed her outings in the wetlands, but even the idea of these trips terrified her. For the first time since she was a small child, Sona watched an entire summer pass without swimming in natural water. Concerned messages came from members of her wild swimming group, but she blocked them without a word, unable to explain.

There were times she felt certain she was losing her grip on reality. Perhaps it was the isolation, but after a few months Sona became convinced that her eyes and mouth were moving on her face. It seemed to her that she was beginning to look more like that poor creature in the observation lab. She might have been able to reassure herself if it weren't for the headaches. Her eye sockets, temples and jaw throbbed with a dull heat. Some days, it felt as if her skull was straining inside a vice, threatening to shatter at any moment.

Still, there was the dream. The blue and yellow clouds, the humming song, and the softly warped vision of the world. In the dream, it was always the same. And while the mud and the river still called, Sona had begun to dread it. Since it first came to her, she had cherished it. Craved it. It had spoken to her of something sweet and beautiful, but now it felt more like a nightmare. She yearned to feel that old feeling of escape and freedom. She hoped that falling asleep would offer some relief from what haunted her days, but these shadows, it seemed, were invading even the deepest parts of her.

The days grew shorter, and as her moulting time approached, Sona began feeling sick and sore. She continued to soak as always but was determined to somehow avoid moulting while under surveillance. It was an irrational thought, of course. She could not stop it. Her fever spiked, and as the familiar lethargic heaviness began to steal into her limbs, her mind clouded. She refused to soak now, hoping to stave off the inevitable. Her body ached and burned with itch.

By the third day, her temperature still high, grey patches of skin hung from attachment sites that swelled and began to look infected. She had nightmares of the woman in the observation lab. Rasping croaking noises reverberated through her bones, and their bodies seemed to melt into each other, until Sona couldn't tell whose form she inhabited.

She struggled to stay conscious and hydrated, but she honestly didn't know what she was trying to accomplish. The moulting had to happen—it would happen. Still, a whisper deep inside told her to resist. Through a haze, she heard a clipped knocking on the door. She hoped desperately whoever it was would just leave without her needing to appear, but the knock came again and then again, more urgently.

Bundled in a blanket, pulled over to the right of her chin to hide a raggedy flap of skin, she looked through the peep hole. A young man in work clothes and a cap stood holding a digital delivery pad, looking distressed. Sona opened the door slightly—cautiously. Without warning, a woman crouching on the ground jerked forward with a long metal stick, sinking a needle deep into Sona's upper thigh.

Too weak to scream, she stumbled backwards into her apartment. Moaning, Sona tried to hold up her hands, any attempt to fight off the invaders useless. In the final flickers of awareness, she saw a small group of people rushing into her home, someone stepping forward to catch her as she fell.

When she came to, she was naked and wrapped in a clean sheet. Its corner was stamped with blocky ink letters, "Department of Zoology." The dusty footprints of hiking boots and fine bits of dried skin littered the floor. Her blanket and clothes appeared to be gone, and her body was red and raw; her skin stung all over. The irritated attachment points, now free from moulting skin, were abraded and treated with some kind of ointment. She felt the place on her thigh where the sedative was injected and moved from there to another sore spot on her right butt cheek. Her fever had broken, but she felt fragile and sluggish. Sona was unable to think about anything beyond sleep, beyond letting go of what she had been fighting for days. Her head throbbed with a pain that buzzed with electric sound. Every joint felt filled with thick sludge. She crawled on her hands and knees, the sheet trailing behind, and heaved herself into bed using all the strength she had left in her body. She slept for the better part of two days; the dream kept its distance.

S ona sat on the train, its steady vibration holding her seething emotions. She knew there was something wrong with her. She had begun to sense it, of course she had. But now she could not avoid the realization that other passengers openly stared at her.

She woke that morning and had slowly gone about a normal routine. Her movements were deliberate, almost meditative, but beneath the surface there was turmoil. Her thoughts were jumbled, difficult to organize, and her vision was still affected. When she tried to focus, the world around her curved and stretched sideways, the details and colours swimming at the centre becoming hyper-vivid. She couldn't grasp onto anything orderly, anything real. She hated herself for it, but she was drawn back to the lab. Compelled by something over which she had no control. She felt consumed by a desire to scream at the professor and his team. It was an empty fury, Sona knew that, but it was the only thing she could clearly identify as her own. She had mad thoughts of kidnapping the other woman. Of running off together somewhere safe. Of destroying the whole place, burning it to the ground. She was as trapped as the poor creature in the lab. If she had any chance at all of putting an end to this and saving herself—saving them both—she had to go back there.

Arriving on campus, Sona bypassed the reception desk

and professors' offices. Going directly to the lab, she pounded on the heavy doors until someone answered. They swung open and there stood the professor, his infuriatingly cheerful face framed by glasses and a scruffy beard. Before she could say a word, he turned and began talking to her over his shoulder, descending the stairs to the observation area.

"Excellent! Excellent!" he cried. "You're up and about."

He ushered Sona to a bank of computers surrounded by a small, buzzing swarm of grad students. Recognizing two of them from her doorway, she took an involuntary step back.

"No, no. No need to run. No one will harm you." The professor softened his voice, almost cooing, and indicated to his students that he wanted Sona to see something. "No doubt you want to know what happened. That will make you feel more relaxed."

As they searched and clicked, acid licked at her throat. *They had filmed it.*

She watched, barely able to breathe, feeling as if her feet were welded to the floor, a small shiver of sparking pain running up and down her limbs. The professor narrated the recording, his voice resonating with excitement while Sona concentrated in order to see what was on the screen, willing her eyes to see.

Looking at herself through the lens of a camera, she felt startled, realizing her face actually had changed.

She absentmindedly touched her jawline as she watched the video, seeing herself being stripped naked and scrubbed. Her temperature was taken, along with four vials of blood. A contraption of long poles with a spring-mounted hook and small boxy device was hastily put together by the team. Sona was rolled, limp and unconscious, onto a sheet, which was then gathered together and attached to the hook. On a count, they hoisted the poles closer together and Sona's body was lifted from the ground, cradled like a bundle. Numbers were read and recorded. It dawned on her that she was being weighed. Pharmaceutical bottles were then removed from a bag and used to fill syringes with large needles. Sona heard the professor say something about vitamins. She watched the needles being plunged into her flesh. Ointment was applied to various spots on her skin, and she was—rather tenderly—swaddled in the sheet. The team had been cleaning up as they went, so there wasn't much left to do but stop the recording.

"You see?" the professor spoke earnestly. All eyes turned to Sona expectantly. "All is well. We were just looking after you. We don't want to lose another specimen."

Sona felt a solemn wave pass over the group. It hit her then. Something was missing. She had been too caught up in her own feelings to examine the absence. Slowly, she moved her gaze in the direction of the observation window. She could see the pond in its entirety and even some of the shore on the level above.

"She died two months ago." The professor's voice took on a soothing tone. "Your readings showed you were in distress. We have to do everything we can to study you and protect your species. Right now, we are monitoring you to see if you would be a good fit for the program."

Numb and cold from too much feeling, Sona turned silently and left the lab. There were whispers behind her, a quick succession of movements and then the sound of humans settling into their relationships with electronic devices. An apprehensive look over her shoulder confirmed what she suspected. For now, they were content to track her from the lab, collecting and indexing data.

Sona kept her actions slow and purposeful. She requested a ride share, waiting on a bench outside the student centre, imagining herself as a tiny blip on a computer screen, holding steady in one place. Once in the car, she relentlessly ignored the driver. The highway murmured beneath the tires.

The car smelled of something artificial, made by people trying to imagine what actual apples and pine needles might smell like. She watched out the window as buildings gave way to guard rails, which melted into trees. She filled herself with visions of the dream, searched for the humming song that overtook her when she was most herself. All the while, she slid her fingers along the smooth metal surface of the tool she carried in her pocket.

She suspected that by the time she arrived, the team at the zoology department would be in their vehicles, preparing to follow her into the wilderness. Possibly sooner, if they figured out where she was going. They may be content to let her roam freely in an urban environment, but once they realized she was heading into the forest, what were the chances they would let her be? She had limited time and only the vaguest idea of what needed to happen.

When they arrived at the trailhead, Sona ran from the vehicle, while the driver called after her about reviews and repeat customers. She pushed hard, climbing deep into the hills as quickly as possible. She knew the trail well, which gave her an advantage, but it was slick with autumn rain and rough going. The sharp tang of pine resin, the edges of the smell blurred by newly mouldering plant matter under the denser patches of growth on either side of the path.

At the river, fractal patterns of early frost clung to the wet rocks. She peeled off her clothes, discarding them in a pile with her phone and wallet. Sweat now growing cold and clammy across her entire body, she squatted for a moment, hands flat on the ground. Hearing the rush of the river behind her, Sona steadied her breathing and reached inside herself for the thing that usually found its way to her. She felt her belly soften, her breathing deepen. Blood rushed into tissues that swelled and loosened in response. She looked down at her hands, nestled in the soil, and saw a tiny shimmer run across the newly scrubbed skin. With a heady mixture of relief and joy, Sona felt the hum begin to rise from her abdomen. Reaching for the utility knife in her jacket pocket, she lifted it to her right ear and quickly, decisively, sliced off the top, tag included.

The pain was iridescent and for an instant Sona felt giddy. Her blood burned with shards of light, her muscles absorbed it, reflecting it back along the nerves to her brain. She inhaled deeply, becoming the sensations that filled her. Sona lifted her face to the sky and let out two croaky calls. Then again and again.

She sent them into the air as she always did, sure only of the need. But this time, they were answered. The moment froze. Sona's mind traced patterns carried on the breeze she'd never noticed before, drenched in spray from the river. There was an absence, a thrilling loss of time and space and story, replaced by immediate experience. Had she really heard it?

Then, they came again. Two calls in quick succession, followed by another two. Sona's blood and skin, her bones, registered those calls as something wondrous and true. They were calls of recognition and welcome. She turned away from the trees and faced the river, scanning the surface of the water, the shoreline, and the forest beyond.

She stood and called again. This time, when the answer came, Sona saw a slight movement of ferns across the river, a tiny shiver in the forest itself. Again. Another response floated clearly from that spot on the opposite shore. Sona focused all of her attention on it, and it appeared to pivot slightly away from her and then back. Suddenly, it moved towards her, shifting into a glimmer of slate grey rocks and ice-cold water as it crossed the river, solidifying into flesh as it climbed the shore to close the distance between them. Only when it was an arm's reach away did she truly comprehend.

There before her stood one of her own kind. Tall and lanky, tawny gold skin veined in murky blue. Hairless, with wide-set eyes the colour of sand. Its elongated mouth stretched back on both sides almost touching its ears, flattened and closed over to near-pinpricks.

It reached up and lightly touched the raw stub of Sona's ear. It vocalized in two warm chirps and traced a line along Sona's jaw, down her neck and chest. A low humming began, punctuated by little groans and burbles, a song that reverberated inside Sona's sternum and sent puddles of thought spreading through her mind. She was too early. Her change, incomplete. She knew it was true, yet she was being

63

welcomed, beckoned, nonetheless.

The creature tensed and looked away into the woods, trilling in clipped, sharp noises. Sona could sense them too. She had known they wouldn't be far behind. It was impossible to tell how close they were, but there wasn't much time. Together, the two of them moved into the river, the creature cooing and humming to Sona when her body began to panic from the cold. Slipping below the surface, she shifted to the use of her gills without a thought, and they sank to a ledge near the bottom of the river's edge. The creature guided her body beneath it and slid against her, wedging them both under the rock. Sona's skin, tight with cold, remained mostly unchanged.

There was a slight shifting of light and dark, places where her outline blurred with her surroundings, but the creature had virtually turned to liquid when entering the water and then crystallized into the deep browns and greys of the rock that hugged them. A blanket of reflected light.

A jolt of fear tore through Sona as the zoology team broke through the forest edge and into the clearing, making their way towards her clothes. They moved slowly and cautiously at first, their activity becoming more rapid and bold as they found her transmitter still clinging to a piece of severed ear. From her hiding place, she could not see them, but she could hear their muffled confusion and distress.

Instinctively, Sona moved a hand to touch her wound.

It was tender, but the blood had completely congealed around the site. Above, someone stepped into the river and Sona jumped; her companion murmured and ran a steadying hand along her waist.

She was unsure how long they stayed beneath the surface. Time ceased to matter. Gradually, the cold seeped into every cell, making her feel heavy and stiff, and a deep shuddering threatened to overwhelm her. As she shook, a soft hum resonated through the creature's torso. Sona concentrated on it, learning to match its rhythm. It did not take long; she began purring along with her companion. Her body temperature stabilized, and small ripples of happiness passed between them. The water around them vibrated placidly, the patterns absorbed by the smooth currents of the river, never disturbing the surface.

The team dispersed and circled back at semi-regular intervals. Sona peered up through the undulating river whenever they approached the shore. She was a world apart from them now, even if she was not complete in her transformation. She was hidden from their view, becoming what she was always intended to be, being made and claimed by this other. And she felt at peace.

As the day drifted towards dusk, the zoology team left. Her companion indicated that they could leave their hiding place, but Sona knew that the site above would not be unmonitored. She struggled to communicate that she, at least, should swim up or down stream before trying to emerge from the water. Whether her companion understood or simply trusted her was unclear, but they went far upstream, following the river into the mountains.

Where they stepped out was not as rocky and woodsy as Sona's usual spot. Here, there were large stretches of mud, damp earth giving rise to scrubby shrubs and thickets. Winter had not yet arrived, but still, it could have looked desolate in the almost faded light. To Sona though, it looked beautiful. She could smell the place where the water and soil merged. Her companion stood beside her, making gentle reassuring sounds while nuzzling softly against her arm and shoulder. Sona's body suddenly seemed ugly and ungainly beside her companion's.

She felt keenly aware of her hair, her monotone skin, her eyes and mouth that were too narrow and her ears, even the partially amputated one, sticking out from her head. Her companion encouraged her to sit. The spot was sheltered by shrubbery behind them and slippery with thick mud. Their feet sunk inches deep as they walked across it, and sitting, Sona felt it embrace her body. Her companion sank her hands into it, scooped great globs of mud onto her fingers, and singing softly, spread it over Sona, beginning at the top of her head. Without knowing exactly why, Sona responded by doing the same for her companion, matching her song, her movements, her breath. They sat for a moment and looked at each other. Forms defined and blurred, covered and revealed. The two creatures entwined their limbs around each other and leaned back, sinking into the mud.

In the dream, it is always the same.

Arria Deepwater is the winner of the 2022 Omnidawn Prize for Fabulist Fiction and the author of "Undertow," published in *In Between Spaces: An Anthology of Disabled Writers* (Stillhouse Press). Arria's work is informed by the deliciously fractured reality of living in a queer disabled body, often exploring themes of grief, authenticity and the spiritual longing for a healed connection between modern society and the natural world. Arria shares a home with her mother, on a beautiful lake in the unceded Omàmiwinini territory known as Eastern Ontario, Canada.

DESCENT
by Arria Deepwater

Cover art by Teagan Berard
Cover typeface: Futura
Interior design by Sophia Carr & Laura Joakimson
Interior typeface: Baskerville

Printed in the United States
by Books International, Dulles, Virginia
Acid Free Archival Quality Recycled Paper

Publication of this book was made possible in part by gifts from
Katherine & John Gravendyk in honor of Hillary Gravendyk,
Francesca Bell, Mary Mackey, and New Place Fund

Staff and Volunteers, Fall 2025
Rusty Morrison & Laura Joakimson, co-publishers
Elizabeth Aeschliman, production editor
Sophia Carr, production editor
Rob Hendricks, poetry & fiction editor
Jeffrey Kingman, copy editor
Hazel White, copy editor
Sharon Zetter, poetry editor & book designer
Anthony Cody, poetry editor
Liza Flum, poetry editor
Jennifer Metsker, marketing assistant
Avantika Chitturi, marketing assistant
Angela Liu, marketing assistant

www.ingramcontent.com/pod-product-compliance
Lightning Source LLC
Chambersburg PA
CBHW010821250626
47156CB00011B/3146